I0766466

My dads are the BEST!

Written by
Steven C. Smith

Illustrated by
Endar Novianto

For information contact:
www.BooksByWordSmith.com
@BooksByWordSmith

Written by Steven C. Smith
With Illustrations by Endar Novianto

978-1-7374690-5-6 Paperback
978-1-7374690-6-3 Hardcover
978-1-0878-9498-0 E-Book

Library of Congress cataloging-in-publication data is available.

My dads are the BEST!

Written by
Steven C. Smith

Illustrated by
Endar Novianto

My family likes to
go to the zoo.

Daddy likes all the beautiful birds.

What a
MESS!
I guess they
like him too.

Birthday parties are so much fun! There are presents, balloons, cake...

...and friends!
We all love to dance!

I think Daddy might
need some more practice.

We like going for
picnics at the park.

Daddy always packs sandwiches and fruit for all of us to share.

Papa likes to feed the ducks.

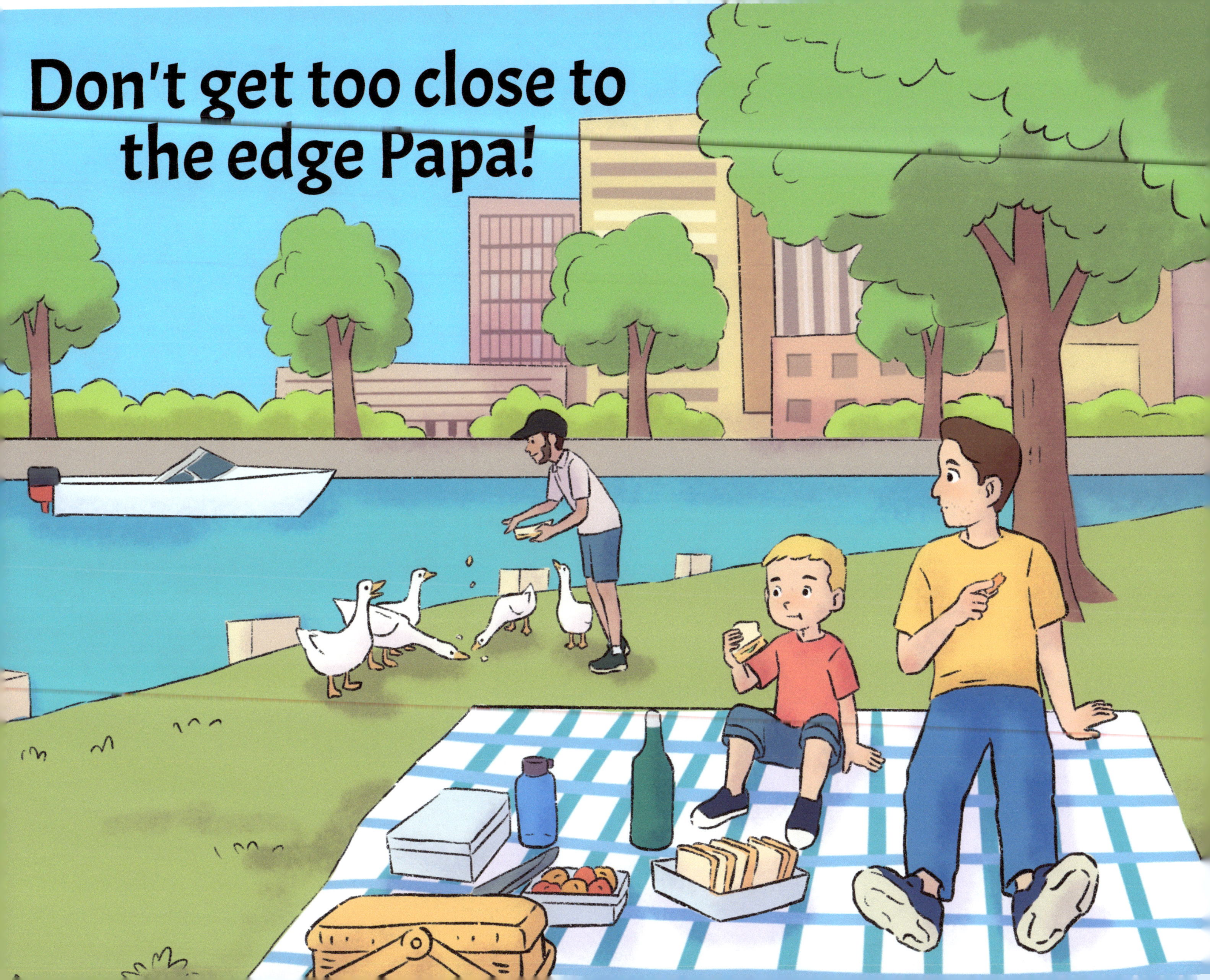
Don't get too close to the edge Papa!

Oh no! Papa fell in.

At Halloween, I love to take my dad's trick-or-treating.

We always wear fun costumes.

They both get spooked so easily...

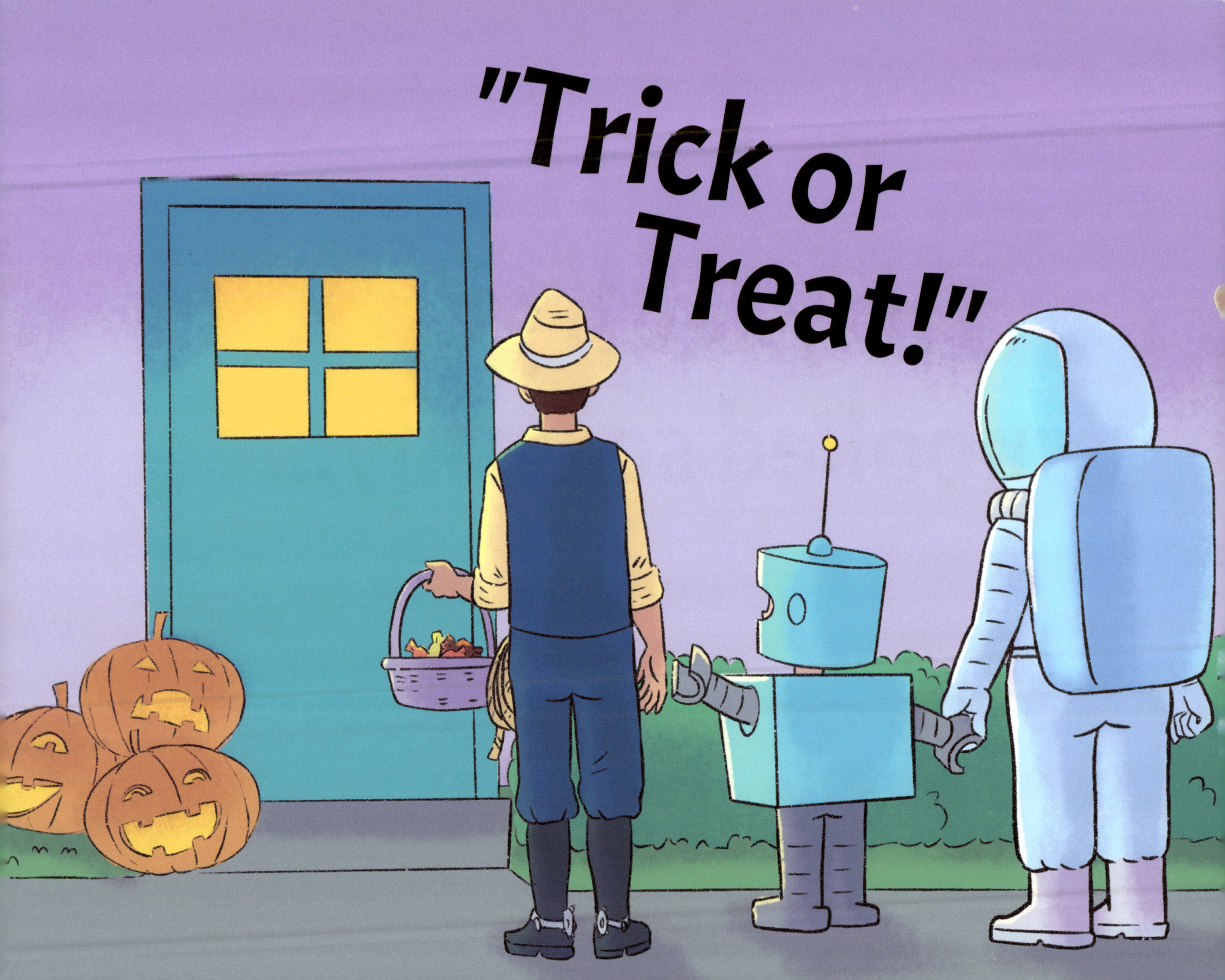

"Trick or Treat!"

I think it's the best.

In the summer,
we like to go
to the beach.

Daddy and I like building fun things in the sand.

Aren't dads the best?

My dads are
BRAVE.

LOVE
makes a family
LOVE IS LOVE

My dads are
KIND.

But, the BEST thing about my dads is...

They're mine!

My dads
are the
BEST!

9 781737 469063